Billy,
the
Condominium
Cat

Billy,
the
Condominium
Cat

Written and Illustrated by

Esphyr Slobodkina

♠ Addison-Wesley

Text and illustrations Copyright © 1980 by Esphyr Slobodkina
All Rights Reserved
Addison-Wesley Publishing Company, Inc.
Reading, Massachusetts 01867
Printed in the United States of America
ABCDEFGHIJK-WZ-89876543210

Library of Congress Cataloging in Publication Data

Slobodkina, Esphyr, 1908–
    Billy, the condominium cat.

    SUMMARY: Billy, an old cat retired with his
mistress to a condominium in Florida, reminisces about
when both he and his mistress were younger.
    [1. Old age—Fiction. 2. Cats—Fiction] I. Ti-
tle.
PZ7.S6334Bj   [E]   79-23402
ISBN 0-201-09204-2

. . . . and now, after many sincere and well
deserved dedications to my loved ones, I think
I can afford this:

*To me, without whom and whose stubborn belief
in my capabilities, none of the twenty books I have
written and illustrated would have been possible.*

Esphyr Slobodkina

Billy, the old cat, lives on the third floor.

He belongs to Bianca who is
also not very young.

Billy and Bianca did not always
live in a third floor apartment
of a Florida condominium built
around a lush tropical garden.

When Billy was a little kitten, he
lived in a nice little house with a
neat little garden, way up north,
in the lovely state of New Hampshire.

When Billy was a little
kitten, there were lots
of sweet-smelling
flowers and happily
smiling children
around him.

There were crocuses and
lilacs in springtime.

There were violets and
roses in summer.

And there were asters
and chrysanthemums
in fall.

But there were no
flowers in winter at all.

In winter there were delightfully naughty
little nephews, and there were cheerfully
bubbly nieces.

They were there in the springtime,
and they were there in the summer.
They were there in the autumn,
but mostly they were
there all through
the winter.

They were there to play games with.

They were there
to cuddle up to.

They were there
to hide from,

and they were
there to give Billy
his supper.

They were there, and they were there
in plenty—to love and to be loved by.

But that was when Billy was a
fluffy, little kitten, and Bianca—
a spry and cheerful Auntie.

Now Bianca was old,
and so was Billy.

Gone was the charming little
house in faraway New Hampshire.

Gone were the naughty, noisy,
laughing nephews and nieces.

Bianca spent most of her time
knitting in the shade of a huge
bougainvillea by the side of a
lovely blue pool or watching TV
in a shaded, air-conditioned
living room.

Billy did not mind it.

It was nice to live in a warm, gentle climate.

He missed the delicious smells of lilacs and roses. But then, he learned to appreciate the heavenly aroma of the orange blossoms and of the Jade flower.

He missed the snow-white winter and often dreamt about it.

But when he woke up, stretching his aching muscles and listening to the creaking of his old bones, he was glad he was in sunny Florida.

But most of all, Billy missed the children.

You see, now that Bianca was old, they moved into a condominium for grown-ups where no children were allowed, except as visitors.

When he did not dream of winter days with white, cold snow on the ground and a bright, warm fire in the fireplace, he dreamt about cool summer days full of wild games with the children and quiet, secluded naps in the shade of the spreading poplars.

Bianca missed them too.

He knew it, for one day she told him it was time to go "home" for a visit.

She packed and prepared for the visit very, very carefully.

Finally they left.

Billy did not like to travel.

He did not like to be shut up in his cat carrier. And he hated to be left alone in the baggage compartment.

Bianca hoped that they would not separate her from Billy.

But they did.

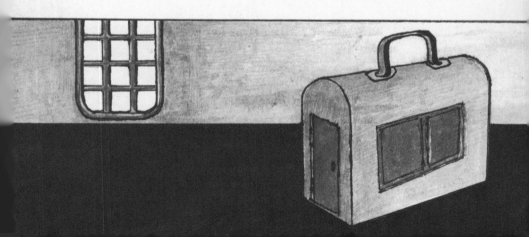

But the plane was fast, and the journey was soon over.

So, as a matter of fact, was the visit.

For, although they were supposed to stay up north for a long, long time, they were back much sooner than they expected.

"It is nice to be visiting, but it is still best to live at home!" said Bianca. And sighing she added a little sadly: "Up north everybody is so busy!"

When they got back, Bianca went visiting with her friends, and Billy went for a slow walk among the oleanders, palms, and Jade flowers.

So, life resumed its normal flow:

They woke up early and tended to their daily duties in the cool of the morning.

They ate and watched TV in the air-conditioned living room.

And they fell asleep and dreamt their dreams, whenever they had nothing else to do.

They dreamt of the days when they were young . . . .

They dreamt of the days when
they were brave . . . .

And they were a little sad when
they woke up and realized that
these were only dreams.

One warm, quiet afternoon,
both of them were asleep
dreaming their dreams.

Billy was slowly moving his tail,
chasing away a particularly naughty,
noisy little boy, and Bianca
was smiling to a chorus of
high-pitched voices asking
her permission to come in.

"Come in! Come in!" said she waking up.

But the voices and the knocking
on the door did not go away.

When Bianca opened the door,
there stood her three youngest nephews
and their mother.

They had come to visit their Aunt
Bianca. They had come to stay for a week.

They swam in the pool,

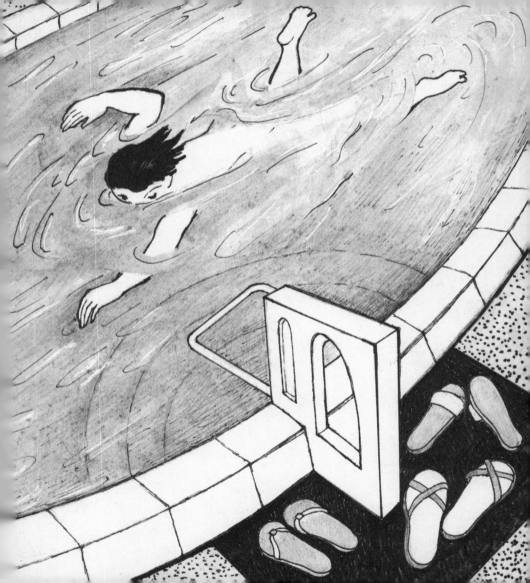

picnicked on the beach,

went to see Disney World,

and they tried to play with Billy.

He caught the dangled cord and obligingly murmured a happy tune when they scratched behind his ear.

After the week was over, they went away.

"That was very, very nice!" sighed Bianca contentedly, lowering herself into a nice, large, comfortable chair.

"That was very nice!" she repeated and closed her tired eyes.

Billy rubbed himself against her legs to show that he understood her, curled up at her feet and went contentedly to sleep.

At 33

Arni (Fritz Glarner)

At 63

Tamara Schildkraut

ESPHYR SLOBODKINA is a multi-talented painter, writer, illustrator and lecturer. She has had more than twenty children's books published, many of which have been reprinted, and her highly acclaimed *Caps for Sale* is considered a modern classic.

Miss Slobodkina was born in that part of Siberia which "was a lovely place to be born in and to spend the first years of one's life, particularly if you were lucky enough to have parents who could provide you with plenty of food, a nice home, warm clothes and lots of fun." The artist's happy childhood is reflected in the delightful books she writes and illustrates for young children.

A founding member of American Abstract Artists and the Federation of Modern Painters and Sculptors, Miss Slobodkina is listed in *Who's Who in American Art.* She has paintings in the permanent collections of The Whitney Museum of American Art, The Corcoran Gallery, the N.Y.U. Permanent Art Collection, the Philadelphia Art Museum and others.

The artist studied at the National Academy of Design and with private tutors. She lives in Great Neck, New York.